Mother Rabbit's Son Tom

by Dick Gackenbach

SCHOLASTIC BOOK SERVICES
NEW YORK · TORONTO · LONDON · AUCKLAND · SYDNEY · TOKYO

For Jim Murphy

ISBN: 0-590-11880-3

12 11 10 9 8 7 6   3 4 5 6 7/8
Printed in the U.S.A.   07

Hamburgers,
Hamburgers

In sweet spring,
Mother Rabbit told Tom,
"Now is the time
to eat the tender dandelions."

"I want a hamburger," said Tom.
"With onions and ketchup
and pickles
on a poppy-seed roll."

Mother Rabbit shook her head.
"Oh dear," she said.
"I wish I had a nickel
for every pickle you eat."

In bright summer,
clover filled the fields.

"Eat some, Tom," Mother Rabbit said.
"The sun has made it
fresh and crisp."

But Tom wanted a hamburger
with onions and ketchup and pickles
on a poppy-seed roll.

"If you eat one more hamburger,"
Mother Rabbit said,
"your tail
will turn into an onion."

Autumn came
and frost filled the air.

Mother Rabbit told Tom,
"Have some good white corn.
It is ripe now."

"No corn!" said Tom.
"I want a hamburger
with onions and ketchup
and pickles
on a poppy-seed roll."

Mother Rabbit
looked into Tom's eyes.
"I thought so," she said.
"Your head is full of ketchup."

Mother Rabbit was worried.
She spoke to Tom's father.
"Someday
our son will turn into
one great big hamburger."

"Yes," said Father Rabbit.
"And his head
will look like
a poppy-seed roll."

In icy winter,
down under the snow,
Mother Rabbit
made a nut-and-berry stew.
"A fine dish for supper,"
she said.

"No thank you," said Tom.

"I know," sighed his mother.
"You want a hamburger!"

"Yes," said Tom.
"With onions and ketchup
and pickles
on a poppy-seed roll."

Early one morning
Mother Rabbit went to wake Tom.
There was a big lump
in his bed.
"What is this?"
she asked.
She peeked under the covers.

"Father!" she called.
"Come as fast as you can."

Father Rabbit
hurried to Tom's bed.

"Look!" said Mother Rabbit.
"Our Tom
has finally turned into
a hamburger!"

"Well," said Father Rabbit.
"What do you think of that?"

"I still love him, though,"
said Mother Rabbit.

"Oh, I do too," said Father Rabbit,
"even if his head
does look like
a poppy-seed roll."

They both laughed.
And Tom laughed most of all.

Tom's Pet

"Mother,
may I keep a dog?"
asked Tom.

"No!"
said his mother.

"I am sorry, Dog,"
said Tom,
"you cannot stay here."

"Mother,"
asked Tom,
"may I keep a cat?"

"You may not,"
said his mother.

"Sorry, Cat,"
said Tom.
"She said no."

"May I keep a chicken, Mother?"
asked Tom.

"No! No! No!" said his mother.

"I cannot have a chicken,"
said Tom.

"Humph!" said Chicken.

"How about a frog?"
asked Tom.

"Please get that thing
out of the house,"
said his mother.

"So long,"
said Tom.
"I do not think
she likes frogs."

"May I keep a dinosaur, Mother?"
asked Tom.

"There are no dinosaurs,"
said his mother.

"If there *were* dinosaurs,
could I keep one?" he asked.
"Yes," laughed his mother,
"you could keep one."